Sybil Gräfin Schönfeldt is the author and translator of numerous children's books, most recently *At the Table with Thomas Mann* (1995) and *Children Need Grandmothers* (1994). She lives in Hamburg.

Born in Bulgaria, Iassen Ghiuselev has illustrated *The Illiad and The Odyssey* (1991), *The Queen Bee* (1994), and *Arthur and Excalibur* (1995).

Orpheus and Eurydice was first published in Germany in 1997 as *Orpheus und Eurydike* by Esslinger Verlag.

Copyright © 1997 by Esslinger Verlag J. F. Scheiber GmbH, Esslingen-Wien, Postfach 10 03 25, 73703 Esslingen (Germany).

English translation © 1996 by Pauline Hejl

First published in the United States of America by the J. Paul Getty Museum, 1200 Getty Center Drive, Suite 1000, Los Angeles, California 90049-1687.

www. getty.edu/publications

Library of Congress Card Number: 00-107828

At the J. Paul Getty Museum:
    Christopher Hudson, *Publisher*
    Mark Greenberg, *Managing Editor*

Project Staff:
    John Harris, *Editor*
    Hillary Sunenshine, *Typographer/Designer*
    Amita Molloy, *Production Coordinator*

Orpheus and Eurydice

By Sybil Gräfin Schönfeldt

Illustrated by Iassen Ghiuselev

Translated by Pauline Hejl

THE J. PAUL GETTY MUSEUM
LOS ANGELES

Orpheus was born in the forest. The first thing he saw was its leaves and above the leaves the bright sky. The first thing he heard was singing. For Orpheus's mother was Calliope, one of the nine muses, and her brother was Apollo, the god of sunshine, music, and poetry. Apollo directed the choir of the muses.

The muses were goddesses. They sang and danced for Orpheus, told him stories, and read his future in the stars.

The muses were related to the nymphs, the shy goddesses who protected the streams and forests. They seldom showed themselves to human beings. Their language was like the murmur of a stream; their songs sounded like the whisper of the wind in the leaves.

Young Orpheus listened to their voices and also to their silence. He tried to sing as softly as the nymphs and as strongly as the muses.

Apollo listened to him, full of pleasure. He taught Orpheus how to fashion the instrument known as a lyre and how to play it. And so Orpheus learned how to make music from the god of music, and from the muses he learned the art of singing.

The voice of Orpheus could
enchant the stones and waterfalls.
His melodies had the power
to make the trees follow him. He
enticed a whole oak forest down
from a mountain with the charm
of his lyre. The oak trees marched
down like soldiers and took root
on the plain.

The wild animals came from far
and wide when they heard Orpheus
singing, and they lay down quietly
at his feet and listened to his song.

When Orpheus roamed through the forests, he often met the tree nymphs. They lived and died with their trees, and just as the nymphs protected their trees from human beings and animals, fire and sickness, so did the trees protect their nymphs.

Orpheus fell in love with an oak nymph. Her name was Eurydice, and she was as beautiful as her oak tree.

Eurydice loved Orpheus and
his singing, and Orpheus loved her.
And so he called to heaven:

Hymen, come and bless our wedding feast!

The god of marriage hurried across
the firmament with his torch.
But before his feet touched the
earth, the bright flame of his
torch began to flicker and grow
dim. That was a bad omen.

Full of joy, Eurydice ran across
the clearing with the other oak
nymphs, toward Hymen. Suddenly
she stepped on a viper, and
the snake bit her heel with its
poison fang.

Eurydice sank to the ground.
She was dead—and Hymen's torch
went out.

Orpheus was overcome with sorrow and began to mourn his beloved Eurydice. He climbed to the top of the highest mountain and played his lyre. His songs were so full of grief that the wind stopped blowing and Apollo darkened the sun. The nymphs fled to their trees, and the trees waved their branches, and the leaves hung down with sorrow.

Orpheus wandered across the
mountains. His lament rose all the
way up to the realm of the wind
and to Zeus himself, the king of
the gods. All the stones rolled out of
his way, and all the wild animals of
the forest followed him and pleaded
to the gods as he did.

Orpheus even wanted to mourn
for Eurydice in the Underworld.
But how could he get there?
Only the dead were led to the
Underworld by Hermes, the
messenger of souls. But Orpheus
was alive.

Who could help him?

The stones and the trees heard his pleas and showed him the way. Orpheus descended into dark and misty regions. He entered gloomy caves, where everything became dim and colors grew pale. Finally he stepped through a stone gate and heard the sound of a river flowing behind the shrouds of mist. It was the Styx, the river surrounding the Underworld.

Near the shore was a boat—it was as if the boat had been waiting

for Orpheus—and Charon the ferryman rowed the singer across the river.

On the other side of the river, Cerberus, the three-headed dog who guarded the entrance to Hades, growled at him suspiciously. It was the job of Cerberus to make sure that none of the shadows ever fled back to the upper world. But now a living person walked past him, and he sang so beautifully that Cerberus forgot to growl.

No one knows how huge the land of shadows is; but one day everyone will find his place there. No one knows where Hades, the god of the Underworld, has his throne, because a magic helmet makes him invisible; but one day everyone will stand before that throne.

Orpheus walked through this silent land full of astonishment. He passed barren fields, through which the river of tears and oblivion flowed. Shadowy beings followed and surrounded him. Many of them had to pay here for their bad deeds.

Orpheus saw Sisyphus, who had betrayed and outwitted the gods. His punishment was that he had to push a huge stone to the top of a mountain, but each time, just before he reached the top, the stone rolled down again. And Orpheus saw Tantalus, who had annoyed the gods. He now had to stand in water that receded every time he tried to drink it, and he was surrounded by fruit trees that were just out of his reach, so that he constantly suffered from hunger and thirst.

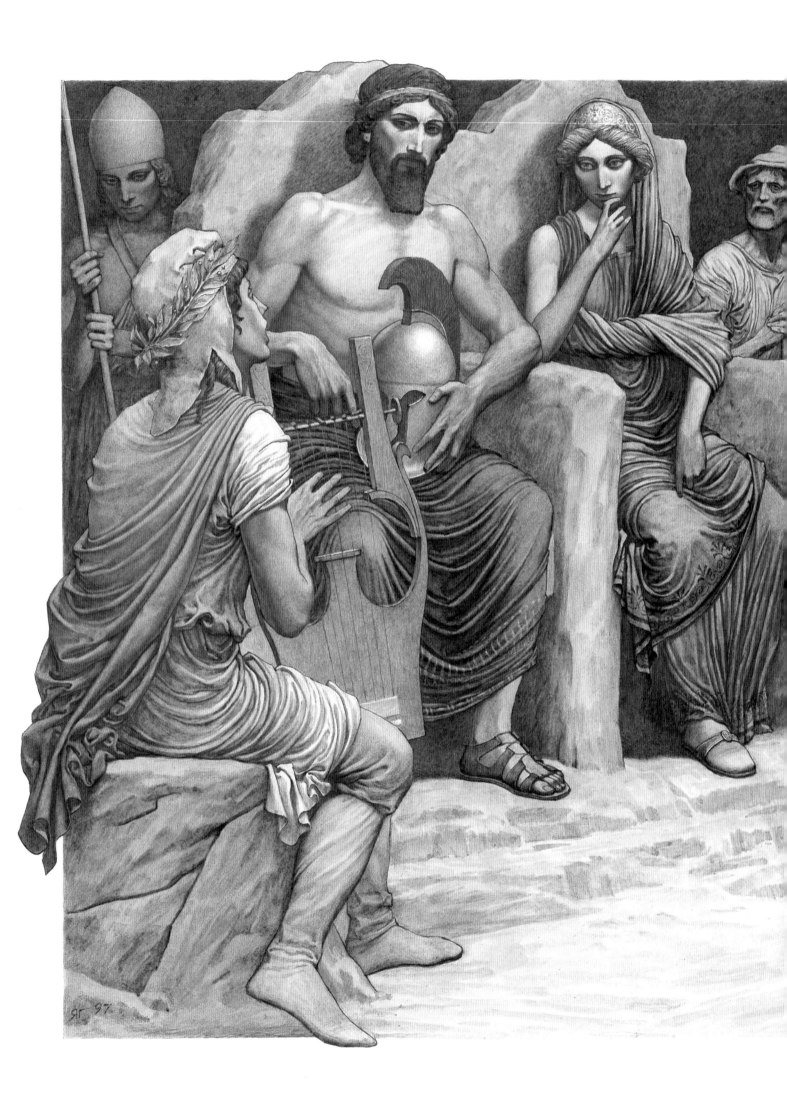

Orpheus once more took his lyre and sang for the gods of the Underworld. He begged them to give him back Eurydice:

I cannot live without her! I know that we all belong to you, and therefore I do not ask you to give her to me forever, only lend her to me. If you cannot grant me this wish, then I do not want to return to the upper world. I prefer to remain in the realm of the dead!

Orpheus sang his plea so beautifully and powerfully that even the dead souls wept.

Hades and the Queen of the Underworld were overpowered by the melodies. They summoned Eurydice. She would have run to Orpheus at the first sound of his voice, but the snakebite still hurt her. Now, accompanied by other shadows, she slowly approached the throne of Hades.

The god had taken off his magic helmet so that he could be seen. He took Eurydice's hand and put it into the hand of Orpheus. Then he spoke:

Down here, in perpetual silence, we have never heard such melodies as yours. Orpheus, take your wife. Hermes, my messenger, will lead you out of our realm. You must go first. But—whatever happens—do not look back at Eurydice. Otherwise she is once more mine!

Orpheus didn't dare to embrace Eurydice: she was as fragile as the other shadows. But when Hermes took her by the hand, more and more life flowed into her with every step she took.

Orpheus went first. The hellhound smiled at him with its three heads. Hermes and the first two mortals ever to leave the realm of the dead were helped by Charon into his boat, and he rowed them to the opposite shore of the Styx, to the shore of the living.

From there they had to climb a mountain, along misty and stony paths. Orpheus didn't look back. He played his lyre and sang and put all his trust in Hermes.

But then he saw the earth and the sunshine before him, and he was overcome with fear that Eurydice might not be able to manage the last steep steps with her injured foot. He forgot that he must not look back, and he turned round lovingly to help her.

She slipped back.

Eurydice stretched out her arms, wanting Orpheus to take hold of her, wanting to hold him her-self, but she was lost. Her arms embraced only the air—and she died for the second time.

Orpheus stood there as if turned to stone. No word of lament left Eurydice's lips, only a last farewell, scarcely to be heard. Then the mist swallowed the shadows of Eurydice and Hermes.

When Orpheus came back to himself, he raced down the gorges to Hades. But Charon had his boat on the other shore of the Styx, on the shore of the dead, and he refused to ferry Orpheus across once more.

For seven days Orpheus remained on the shore of the Styx. He could neither sing nor eat, and all he drank was his tears.

Then he returned home, where he mourned for Eurydice for three years. His songs became even more beautiful because of his longing. People stopped what they were doing and followed Orpheus, wanting to hear more from him and to learn from him.

And that is how singing came into the world.